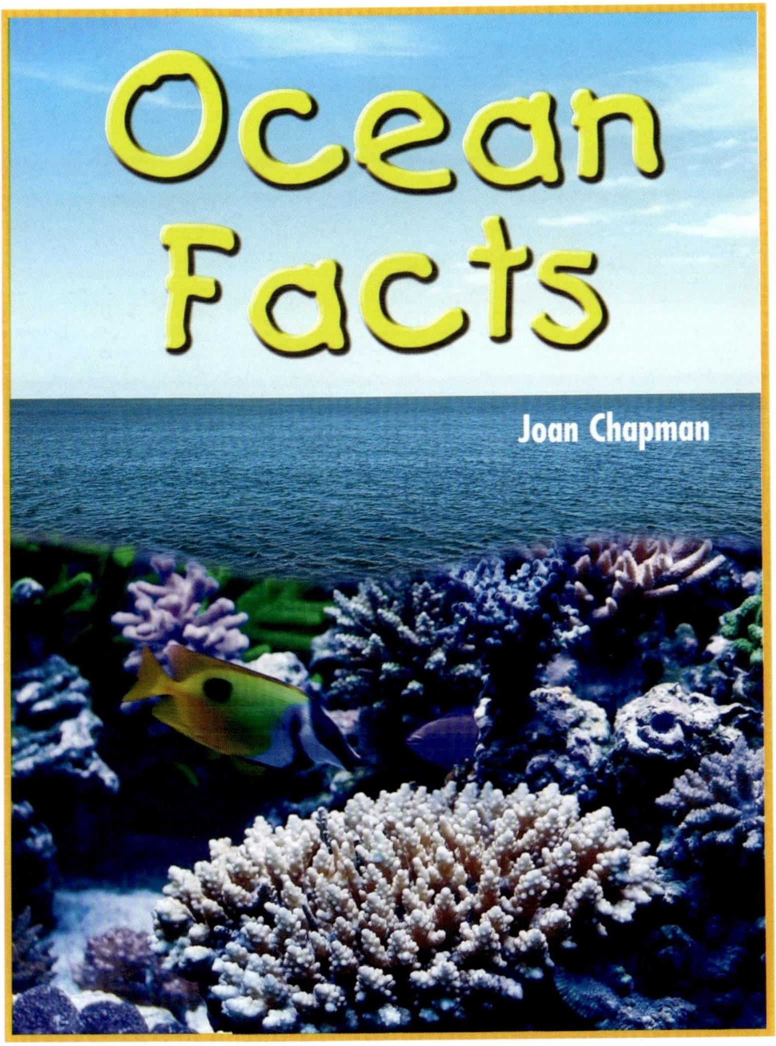

Rosen REAL READERS

The Rosen Publishing Group, Inc.
New York

Oceans are full of salt water.

Many kinds of fish live in the ocean.

Sharks live in the ocean.

Whales live in the ocean.

Many kinds of plants live in the ocean.

People can swim and play in the ocean.

Words to Know

fish

ocean

people

plants

sharks

whales